Katy Cares for the Animals

Katherine Bailey

Katherine Bailey

PublishingWorks, Inc.
2008

Copyright © 2008 by Katherine Bailey. All rights reserved.

All rights reserved. No part of this book may be reproduced or transmitted in any form or by any means, electronic or mechanical, including photocopying, recording, or by an information storage and retrieval system—except by a reviewer who may quote brief passages in a review to be printed in a magazine or newspaper—without permission in writing from the publisher.

PublishingWorks, Inc.,
60 Winter Street
Exeter, NH 03833
603-778-9883
For Sales and Orders:
1-800-738-6603 or 603-772-7200

ISBN-13: 978-1-933002-96-5

Printed by Stillwater Graphics, Williamstown, Vermont,
using elemental chlorine-free paper and soy-based ink.

for Him –
Who makes cats and dogs,
ponies and cows,
bunnies and birds,
boys and girls,
and snow

"All things were created through him and for him"
Colossians 1:16 ESV

Katy is a kind tenderhearted dog.
She is a dog with responsibilities.
She lives on a farm in Lyme, New Hampshire.

Three times a day Katy checks on the farm animals.
Are they safe? Are they warm?
Do they have enough to eat?
Katy will find out.

Time to go!

Katy is ready.
Molly, the golden cocker spaniel is ready.
Alice, Molly's puppy, and Queenie,
the gray cat are ready.

But is Skyler ready?

Snow is falling – one flake, two flakes, hundreds of flakes.
Will snow stop Katy?
No! She has a job to do.

First, the birdfeeder.
How are the chickadees, the red cardinal,
and the gray squirrel?
All the berries and nuts are gone, but they are
feasting on sunflower seeds.

Next, the rabbit hutch.
Skyler gives Chocolate and Clara Bell
a crisp carrot for breakfast.
Crunch. Crunch. Crunch.
They share the treat.

Thank you, Skyler.

Down the hill, past the barn –
Charlie, the white-faced Hereford calf,
sticks his head through the fence.
He wants Skyler to scratch his little poll.
Oh, that feels good!

The white pony and the brown mare
are eating their morning feed.

After lunch it is time for Katy to make her rounds again.
Skyler puts on his red hat and mittens.
Out the door go Katy and her helpers.

Gray squirrel visits with them from the birdfeeder.
Skyler eats a snowball.
Brrr – it makes his teeth cold!

Scrunch. Scrunch. Scrunch.
The cold snow squeaks as they walk.
Clara Bell and Chocolate are watching snowflakes fall.

Katy and her helpers feed apples
to Charlie, the brown mare,
and the white pony.

What a treat!
Thank you!

Katy and her friends are having a good afternoon.

Now it is time to say goodnight to the animals,
but Queenie is still sleeping.
Wake up kitty.
It is time to go.

Whoo! Whoo! Howls the wind.

Everyone wears a scarf.
Out they go into the cold.

The birdfeeder has on a marshmallow hat.
Red Cardinal is nesting high in the tree.
Curled up in his hole, Gray Squirrel sleeps
under his fluffy tail.
Can you find the chickadees
tucked-up under the branches?

Sleep tight, Gray Squirrel.
Sleep tight, Chickadees.
Sleep tight, Red Cardinal.

The cold wind cannot find
Clara Bell and Chocolate;
The snow keeps their home
snug and warm.

Sleep tight, Clara Bell.
Sleep tight, Chocolate.

Charlie is cozy between the white pony
and the brown mare.
They are sleeping under a blanket of snow.

Sleep tight, Charlie.
Sleep tight, White Pony.
Sleep tight, Brown Mare.

Up the hill through the deep snow
trudge Katy, Molly and Alice.
Up the hill trudge Queenie and Skyler.

Katy and her helpers have had a busy day.
They have done a good job.

Sleep tight, Katy.
Sleep tight, Molly.
Sleep tight, Alice and Queenie.
Sleep tight, Skyler.

God Bless You.

STORY FIGURES

Color, cut out, cover with clear paper and *PLAY!*

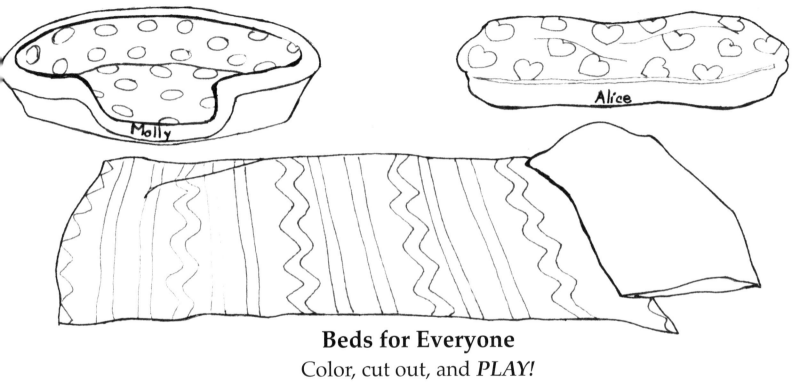

Molly

Alice

Beds for Everyone

Color, cut out, and *PLAY!*

Katy

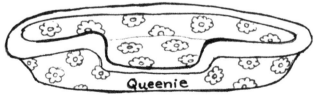

Queenie

About the Author

In writing and illustrating *Katy Cares for the Animals*, Katherine Bailey drew on much that is familiar to her. She grew up on a farm in Vermont, and now lives with her husband on a little farm in Lyme, New Hampshire. Katy, Molly, and Queenie live with them, and Alice, who really is Molly's puppy, visits nearly every day. All the other animals in the story have also lived on the Bailey Farm, and Skyler is one of Katherine's grandchildren.